Rocky
the Robot *Helps Out*

by Lucinda Cotter

Illustrated by Dylan Gibson

raintree

a Capstone company — publishers for children

Engage Literacy is published in the UK by Raintree.
Raintree is an imprint of Capstone Global Library Limited, a company incorporated in England and Wales
having its registered office at 264 Banbury Road, Oxford, OX2 7DY – Registered company number: 6695582

www.raintree.co.uk

Text copyright © Capstone 2017

Illustration copyright Capstone/Dylan Gibson

Editorial credits
Gina Kammer, editor; Cynthia Della-Rovere, designer; Tori Abraham, production specialist

10 9 8 7 6 5 4 3 2 1
Printed and bound in China.

Rocky the Robot Helps Out

ISBN: 978 1 4747 3160 7

Contents

Chapter 1
Help wanted!

"Oh no, not again!" shouted Dad, looking worried.

Tamal looked up from the book he was reading. He watched as Dad dropped the vacuum cleaner and ran from the room towards the kitchen.

A cloud of smoke floated through the door towards him. Maybe the house was on fire! Tamal quickly dropped his book and ran after Dad.

There stood Dad by the open oven holding a big black lump in a tin. The kitchen was full of smoke.

"That's the second cake I have burned this week," grumbled Dad, looking very sad.

Mum opened the window. She flapped at the thick smoke with a tea towel. "That's because you are trying to do too many things at once," she said quietly.

"I know," replied Dad. "But with my part-time job and looking after the house, there just isn't enough time." He dropped the burned lump onto the table. "What we all need is a full-time helper. Wouldn't it be wonderful to have a robot to help with the housework? Then we would all have plenty of time to do the things we love."

Mum laughed. "It's a nice thought," she said. "But I suppose we'll all just have to do our part to help with the housework." She handed the towel to Tamal. "Come on, then. You clear the smoke while I help Dad with the dishes."

Chapter 2
Help arrives

The next day, the doorbell rang. Dad went to answer it, but when he opened the front door, nobody was standing there. Instead when he looked down, he found an enormous cardboard box sitting on the doorstep. But when he tried to pick it up, it made a weird noise.

Bzzzzzz! Bzzzzzz! Brrrrrr!

Dad quickly jumped back. This was no ordinary box!

Suddenly, the box moved. Slowly, it began to rise up, higher and higher. Dad saw that the box had cardboard legs, tube arms and a head!

Bzzzzzz! Bzzzzzz! Brrrrr!

"I am Rocky the Robot," it said in a robot voice. "I am here to assist you."

"Well, you'd better come in, then," said Dad with a big smile on his face.

Bzzzzzz! Bzzzzzz! Brrrrr!

Rocky the Robot marched forward through the front door and into the living room. "Your wish is my command," said Rocky. "How may I assist you?"

Dad thought for a moment. "Well, I could use some help vacuuming the carpets."

"I will do as you command," buzzed Rocky. He marched to the hall cupboard and dragged out the vacuum cleaner. Dad plugged it in, and away Rocky went.

"I suppose I'll go and do something else, then," said Dad, and he left Rocky to his vacuuming.

Chapter 3
Not so helpful!

CRASH! BANG!

Dad came running to the living room. There he found Rocky the Robot sitting on the floor. The cord of the vacuum cleaner was wrapped tightly around his robot legs.

Dad tried not to laugh as he helped Rocky get up. "Maybe vacuuming isn't the right job for a robot," he suggested. "We had better find you something else to help with."

"I will do as you command," said Rocky. "How may I assist you?"

"It's been ages since anyone has dusted the shelves," replied Dad.

Rocky the Robot marched to the hall cupboard and got out the fluffy duster.

Bzzzzzz! Bzzzzzz! Brrrrrr!

He set to work quickly dusting the shelves while Dad went back to baking in the kitchen.

BANG! CRASH!

This time when Dad came running, he found a broken vase with its pieces all over the living room floor.

Rocky the Robot hung his robot head. "Rocky is very, very sorry," he said in his robot voice. "It was an accident."

Dad sighed. "Never mind, Rocky. I didn't really like that thing, anyway." He picked up the broken pieces and put them in the bin. "Let's find you something else to help with."

Chapter 4
Try and try again

So far Rocky the Robot hadn't had much luck being a helper. But he still kept trying.

When Dad asked him to hang out the washing, his robot arms couldn't reach the clothesline.

When he tried to water the potted plants, he watered his robot shoes instead.

When Rocky tried to clean the bath, he fell in, and his robot parts got all soggy. Whatever he tried to do to help, it just seemed to go wrong.

"Rocky the Robot has failed," he said in a sad robot voice. "Rocky will leave now." He hung his robot head and slowly marched towards the front door.

Chapter 5
One more job

"Not so fast!" called Dad. He hurried over to Rocky and took him by the robot hand. He marched Rocky into the kitchen and over to the table. "I have one more job for you to try."

Dad pointed to the mixing bowl on the table. "I'm making a banana cake, but I need your help to stir the mixture," he said. "My arms are getting tired. But it should be easy for a strong robot like you."

"I will do as you command," said Rocky happily. "I will assist you." He picked up the wooden spoon and began to stir the mixture. He stirred and stirred until it was really well mixed. Then he poured the mixture into a tin.

Wearing oven gloves, Rocky carefully put the cake tin into the oven. Then he set the timer for 30 minutes.

When the cake was baked and cooled, he spread the lemon icing on top and sprinkled it with some coconut.

"Thanks, Rocky! You've been a great help," said Dad.

"As you command," said Rocky. "Happy to assist you."

Dad got out two plates. He cut two pieces of the banana cake and put them on the plates. But then he looked sadly at Rocky.

"What is the matter?" asked Rocky in his robot voice. "Did Rocky do something wrong?"

"No," replied Dad. "It's not that. It's just a shame that robots don't eat. It would be nice if we could share the cake after all your help today. But that would be impossible, wouldn't it?"

Suddenly, Rocky the Robot began to shake.

Bzzzzzzz! Bzzzzzz! Brrrrrr! Rrrrrrrrrrip!

Off came Rocky's robot head. Off came his
robot arms and legs. Rip went Rocky's robot body.

"SURPRISE!" said Tamal. He ran over and gave Dad a giant hug.

"Look who's back!" he said. "And just in time to eat banana cake!"

Tamal sat at the table and picked up his piece of cake. "I will do as you command!" he said before taking a huge bite.